The
Little Cookie

Modern Curriculum Press
BEGINNING
TO
READ
Series

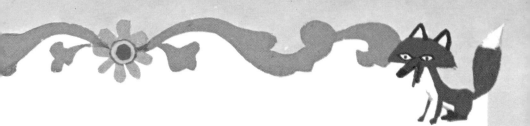

The
Little Cookie

Margaret Hillert
Illustrated by Donald Charles

MODERN CURRICULUM PRESS

ISBN: 0-8136-5562-5 (paperback)
ISBN: 0-8136-5062-3 (hardbound)

Printed in the United States of America
18 19 20 21   07 06 05

Modern
Curriculum
Press

Pearson Learning Group

1-800-821-3106
www.pearsonlearning.com

See me work.
I can make something.
I can make a cookie,
a funny little cookie.

6

Look, look.
See the funny cookie.
It is little.

Oh, look.
See it go.
It can run and jump.
It can run away.

No, no, little cookie.
Come here. Come here.
I want you.

No, no.
See me go.
I can run and play.
I can run away.
You can not get me.

It is fun to run.
It is fun to play.
I can run, run, run.
I can run away.

I can go up.

I can go down.
Away, away, away.

Cookie, cookie.
Come here.
Come here to me.
I want you.

No, no.
See me go.
I can run and play.
I can run away.
You can not get me.

Look up, cookie.
Look up here.
Come to me.
I want you.

No, no.
See me go.
I can run and play.
I can run away.
You can not get me.

Look down, cookie.
Look down here.
Come into my house.
I want you.

18

No, no.
See me go.
I can run and play.
I can run away.
You can not get me.

20

Cookie, cookie.
See big me.
I want you.
Come here to me.

21

No, no.
See me go.
I can run and play.
I can run away.
You can not get me.

Come here, little cookie.
I want you.
Run, run, run.
24 Run here to me.

No, no.
See me go.
I can run and play.
I can run away.
You can not get me.

Oh, my.
I can not go here.
I can not go in here.

Come to me, little cookie.
I can help you.
I can go in.

One, two, three.
Here we go!

Oh, no! Oh, no!
Look at me now.
What is this?
This is not good.
No, this is not good!

Margaret Hillert, author of several books in the MCP Beginning-To-Read Series, is a writer, poet, and teacher.

The Little Cookie uses the 48 words listed below.

a	get	make	the
and	go	me	this
at	good	my	three
away			to
	help	no	two
big	here	not	
	house	now	up
can			
come	I	oh	want
cookie	in	one	we
	into		what
down	is	play	work
	it		
fun		run	you
funny	jump		
		see	
	little	something	
	look		